'The valley was full of snakes and serpents as big as palm trees, so huge that they could have swallowed any elephant that met them...'

This selection of stories is taken from the collection of seven stories entitled *Sindbad the Sailor* from *Tales from 1,001 Nights*, Penguin Classics, 2010. *Tales from 1,001 Nights* is an abridged version of the three volumes published by Penguin Classics 2008.

ARABIAN NIGHTS IN PENGUIN CLASSICS

The Arabian Nights: Tales of 1,001 Nights (Volume I)
The Arabian Nights: Tales of 1,001 Nights (Volume II)
The Arabian Nights: Tales of 1,001 Nights (Volume III)
Tales from 1,001 Nights
Three Tales from the Arabian Nights

ANONYMOUS

Sindbad the Sailor

Translated by
Malcolm C. Lyons

PENGUIN BOOKS

PENGUIN CLASSICS

Published by the Penguin Group
Penguin Books Ltd, 80 Strand, London WC2R ORL, England
Penguin Group (USA) Inc., 375 Hudson Street, New York, New York 10014, USA
Penguin Group (Canada), 90 Eglinton Avenue East, Suite 700, Toronto, Ontario, Canada M4P 2Y3 (a division of Pearson Penguin Canada Inc.)
Penguin Ireland, 25 St Stephen's Green, Dublin 2, Ireland (a division of Penguin Books Ltd)
Penguin Group (Australia), 707 Collins Street, Melbourne, Victoria 3008, Australia (a division of Pearson Australia Group Pty Ltd)
Penguin Books India Pvt Ltd, 11 Community Centre, Panchsheel Park, New Delhi – 110 017, India
Penguin Group (NZ), 67 Apollo Drive, Rosedale, Auckland 0632, New Zealand (a division of Pearson New Zealand Ltd)
Penguin Books (South Africa) (Pty) Ltd, Block D, Rosebank Office Park, 181 Jan Smuts Avenue, Parktown North, Gauteng 2193, South Africa

Penguin Books Ltd, Registered Offices: 80 Strand, London WC2R ORL, England

www.penguin.com

This selection published in Penguin Classics 2015
002

Set in 10/14.5 pt Baskerville 10 Pro
Typeset by Jouve (UK), Milton Keynes
Printed in Great Britain by Clays Ltd, St Ives plc

A CIP catalogue record for this book is available from the British Library

ISBN: 978-0-141-39768-9

www.greenpenguin.co.uk

Penguin Books is committed to a sustainable future for our business, our readers and our planet. This book is made from Forest Stewardship Council™ certified paper.

Contents

Sindbad the Sailor

In the time of the caliph Harun al-Rashid, the Commander of the Faithful, there was in the city of Baghdad a man called Sindbad the porter, a poor fellow who earned his living by carrying goods on his head. On one particularly hot day he was tired, sweating and feeling the heat with a heavy load, when he passed by the door of a merchant's house. The ground in front of it had been swept and sprinkled with water and a temperate breeze was blowing. As there was a wide bench at the side of the house, he set down his bundle in order to rest there and to sniff the breeze.

From the door came a refreshing breath of air and a pleasant scent which attracted him, and as he sat he heard coming from within the house the sound of stringed instruments and lutes, together with singing and clearly chanted songs. In addition, he could hear birds twittering and praising God Almighty in all their varied tongues – turtledoves, nightingales, thrushes, bulbuls, ringdoves and curlews. He wondered at this and, filled as he was with pleasure, he moved forward and discovered within the grounds of the house a vast orchard in which he could see pages, black slaves, eunuchs, retainers and so forth, such as are only to be found in the palaces of kings and sultans. When he smelt the scent of all kinds of appetizing foods, together with fine wines, he looked up to heaven and said: 'Praise be to You, my Lord, Creator and Provider, Who sustains those whom You wish beyond all reckoning. I ask You to forgive all my sins, and I repent of my faults to You. My Lord, none can oppose Your judgement or power, or question Your acts, for You are omnipotent, praise be to You. You make one man rich and another poor, as You choose; You exalt some and humble others in accordance with Your will and there is no other god but You. How great You are! How strong is Your power and how excellent is Your governance! You show favour to those of Your servants whom You choose, for here is the owner of this house living in the greatest prosperity, enjoying pleasant scents, delicious food and all kinds of splendid wines. You have decreed what You wish with regard to your servants in accordance with Your power. Some are worn out and others live at ease; some are fortunate while others, like me, live laborious and humble lives.'

He then recited these lines:

How many an unfortunate, who has no rest,
Comes later to enjoy the pleasant shade.
But as for me, my drudgery grows worse,
And so, remarkably, my burdens now increase.
Others are fortunate, living without hardship,
And never once enduring what I must endure.
They live in comfort all their days,
With ease and honour, food and drink.
All are created from a drop of sperm;
I'm like the next man and he is like me,
But oh how different are the lives we lead!
How different is wine from vinegar.
I do not say this as a calumny;
God is All-Wise and His decrees are just.

When Sindbad the porter had finished these lines, he was about to pick up his load and carry it off when a splendidly dressed young boy, well proportioned and with a handsome face, came through the door, took his hand and said: 'Come and have a word with my master, for he invites you in.' Sindbad wanted to refuse, but finding that impossible, he left his load with the gatekeeper in the entrance hall and entered. He found an elegant house with an atmosphere of friendliness and dignity, and there he saw a large room filled with men of rank and importance. It was decked out with all kinds of flowers and scented herbs; there were fruits both dried and fresh, together with expensive foods of all kinds as well as wines of rare vintages; and there were musical instruments played by beautiful slave girls of various races. Everyone was seated in his appointed place and at their head was a large and venerable man whose facial hair was touched with grey. He was handsome and well shaped, with an imposing air of dignity, grandeur and pride. Sindbad the porter was taken aback, saying to himself: 'By God, this is one of the regions of Paradise, or perhaps the palace of a king or a sultan.' Then, remembering his manners, he greeted the company, invoking blessings on them and kissing the ground before them.

He stood there with his head bowed in an attitude of humility until the master of the house gave him permission to sit and placed him on a chair near his own, welcoming him and talking to him in a friendly way before offering him some of the splendid, delicious and expensive foods that were there. The porter, after invoking the Name of God, ate his fill and then exclaimed: 'Praise be to God in all things!' before washing his hands and thanking the company. The master of the house, after again welcoming him and wishing him good fortune, asked his name and his profession. 'My name is Sindbad the porter,' his guest replied, 'and in return for a fee I carry people's goods on my head.' The master smiled and said: 'You must know, porter, that your name is the same as mine, and I am Sindbad the sailor. I would like you to let me hear the verses which you were reciting as you stood at the door.' Sindbad the porter was embarrassed and said: 'For the sake of God, don't hold this against me, for toil and hardship together with a lack of means teach a man bad manners and stupidity.' 'Don't be ashamed,' said his host. 'You have become a brother to me, so repeat the verses that I admired when I heard you recite them at the door.' Sindbad the porter did this, moving Sindbad the sailor to delighted appreciation, after which THIS SECOND SINDBAD SAID:

The Valley of Diamonds

I was enjoying a life of the greatest pleasure and happiness until one day I got the idea of travelling to foreign parts, as I wanted to trade, to look at other countries and islands and to earn my living. After I had thought this over, I took out a large sum of money and bought trade goods and other things that would be useful on a voyage. I packed these up and when I went down to the coast I found a fine new ship with a good set of sails, fully manned and well equipped. A number of other merchants were there and they and I loaded our goods on board. We put to sea that day and had a pleasant voyage, moving from one sea and one island to another, and wherever we anchored we were met by the local traders and dignitaries as well as by buyers and sellers, with whom we bought, sold and bartered our goods.

Things went on like this until fate brought us to a

pleasant island, full of trees with ripe fruits, scented flowers, singing birds and limpid streams, but without any houses or inhabitants. The captain anchored there and the merchants, together with the crew, disembarked to enjoy its trees and its birds, giving praise to the One Omnipotent God, and wondering at His great power. I had gone with this landing party and I sat down by a spring of clear water among the trees. I had some food with me and I sat there eating what God had provided for me; there was a pleasant breeze; I had no worries and, as I felt drowsy, I stretched out at my ease, enjoying the breeze and the delightful scents, until I fell fast asleep. When I woke up, there was no one to be found there, human or *jinn*. The ship had sailed off leaving me, as not a single one on board, merchants or crew, had remembered me. I turned right and left, and when I failed to find anyone at all, I fell into so deep a depression that my gall bladder almost exploded through the force of my cares, sorrow and distress. I had no possessions, no food and no drink; I was alone, and in my distress I despaired of life. I said to myself: 'The pitcher does not always remain unbroken. I escaped the first time by meeting someone who took me with him from the island to an inhabited part, but this time how very,

very unlikely it is that I shall meet anyone to bring me to civilization!'

I started to weep and wail, blaming myself in my grief for what I had done, for the voyage on which I had embarked, and for the hardships I had inflicted on myself after I had been sitting at home in my own land at my ease, enjoying myself and taking pleasure in eating well, drinking good wine and wearing fine clothes, in no need of more money or goods. I regretted having left Baghdad to go to sea after what I had had to endure on my first voyage, which had brought me close to death. I recited the formula: 'We belong to God and to Him do we return,' and I was close to losing my reason. Then I got up and began to wander around, not being able to sit still in any one place. I climbed a high tree and from the top of it I started to look right and left, but all I could see was sky, water, trees, birds, islands and sand. Then, when I stared more closely, I caught sight of something white and huge on the island. I climbed down from my tree and set out to walk towards it. On I went until, when I reached it, I found it to be a white dome, very tall and with a large circumference. I went nearer and walked around it but I could find no door and the dome itself was so smoothly polished that I had neither the strength nor the agility to climb it. I marked my starting point and made a circuit of it to measure its circumference, which came to fifty full paces, and then I started to think of some way to get inside it.

It was coming on towards evening. I could no longer see the sun, and the sky had grown dark; I thought that the sun must have been hidden by a cloud, but since it was summer I found this surprising and I raised my head to look again. There, flying in the sky, I caught sight of an enormous bird with a huge body and broad wings. It was this that had covered the face of the sun, screening its rays from the island. I was even more amazed, but I remembered an old travellers' tale of a giant bird called the *rukh* that lived on an island and fed its chicks on elephants, and I became sure that my 'dome' was simply a *rukh*'s egg. While I was wondering at what Almighty God had created, the parent bird flew down and settled on the egg, covering it with its wings and stretching its legs behind it on the ground. It fell asleep – glory be to God, Who does not sleep – and I got up and undid my turban, which I folded and twisted until it was like a rope. I tied this tightly round my waist and attached myself as firmly as

I could to the bird's legs in the hope that it might take me to a civilized region, which would be better for me than staying on the island.

I spent the night awake, fearful that if I slept, the bird might fly off before I realized what was happening. When daylight came, it rose from the egg and with a loud cry it carried me up into the sky, soaring higher and higher until I thought that it must have reached the empyrean. It then began its descent and brought me back to earth, settling on a high peak. As soon as it had landed I quickly cut myself free from its legs, as I was afraid of it, although it hadn't noticed that I was there. I was trembling as I undid my turban, freeing it from the bird's legs, and I then walked off, while, for its part, the bird took something in its talons from the surface of the ground and then flew back up into the sky. When I looked to see what it had taken, I discovered that this was a huge snake with an enormous body. I watched in wonder as it left with its prey, and I then walked on further, to find myself on a high ridge under which there was a broad and deep valley, flanked by a vast and unscalable mountain that towered so high into the sky that its summit was invisible. I blamed myself for what I had done and wished that I had stayed on the island, saying to myself: 'That was better than this barren place, as there were various kinds of fruits to eat and streams from which to drink, whereas here there are no trees, fruits or streams.' I recited the formula: 'There is no power and no might except with God, the Exalted, the Almighty,' adding: 'Every time I escape from one disaster, I fall into another that is even worse.'

I got up and, plucking up my courage, I walked down into the valley, where I discovered that its soil was composed of diamonds, the hard and compact stone that is used for boring holes in metals, gems, porcelain and onyx. Neither iron nor rock has any effect on it; no part of it can be cut off and the only way in which it can be broken is by the use of lead. The valley was full of snakes and serpents as big as palm trees, so huge that they could have swallowed any elephant that met them, but these only came out at night and hid away by day for fear of *rukhs* and eagles, lest they be carried away and torn in bits, although I don't know why that should be. I stayed there filled with regret at what I had done, saying to myself: 'By God, you have hastened your own death.' As evening drew on, I walked around looking for a place where I could spend the night, and I was so afraid of the snakes that in my concern for my safety I forgot about eating and drinking. Nearby I spotted a cave and when I approached it, I found that its entrance was narrow. I went into it and then pushed a large stone that I found nearby in order to block it behind me. 'I'm safe in here,' I told myself, 'and when day breaks I shall go out and see what fate brings me.'

At that point I looked inside my cave only to see a huge snake asleep over its eggs at the far end. All the hairs rose on my body and, raising my head, I entrusted myself to fate. I spent a wakeful night, and when dawn broke I removed the stone that I had used to block the entrance and came out, staggering like a drunken man through the effects of sleeplessness, hunger and fear. Then, as I was walking, suddenly, to my astonishment, a large carcass fell in front of me, although there was no one in sight. I thought of a travellers' tale that I had heard long ago of the dangers of the diamond mountains and of how the only way the diamond traders can reach these is to take and kill a sheep, which they skin and cut up. They then throw it down from the mountain into the valley and, as it is fresh when it falls, some of the stones there stick to it. The traders leave it until midday, at which point eagles and vultures swoop down on it and carry it up to the mountain in their talons. Then the traders come and scare them away from the flesh by shouting at them, after which they go up and remove the stones that are sticking to it. The flesh is left for the birds and beasts and the stones are taken back home by the traders. This is the only way in which they can get hold of the diamonds.

I looked at the carcass and remembered the story. So I went up to it and cleared away a large number of diamonds which I put in my purse and among my clothes, while I stored others in my pockets, my belt, my turban and elsewhere among my belongings. While I was doing this, another large carcass fell down and, lying on my back, I set it on my breast and tied myself to it with my turban, holding on to it and lifting it up from the ground. At that point an eagle came down and carried it off into the air in its talons, with me fastened to it. The eagle flew up to the mountain top where it deposited the carcass, and it was about to tear at it when there came a loud shout from behind it, together with the noise of sticks striking against rocks. The eagle took fright and flew off, and, having freed myself from the carcass, I stood there beside it, with my clothes all smeared with blood. At that point the trader who had shouted at the eagle came up, but when he saw me standing there he trembled and was too afraid of me to speak. He went to the carcass and turned it over, giving a great cry of disappointment and reciting the formula: 'There is no might and no power except with God. We take refuge with God from Satan, the accursed.' In his regret he struck the palms of his hands together, exclaiming: 'Alas, alas, what is this?'

I went up to him, and when he asked me who I was and why I had come there, I told him: 'Don't be afraid. I am a mortal man, of good stock, a former merchant. My story is very remarkable indeed, and there is a strange tale attached to my arrival at this mountain and this valley. There is no need for you to be frightened, for I have enough to make you happy – a large number of diamonds, of which I will give what will satisfy you, and each of my stones is better than anything else that you can get. So don't be unhappy or alarmed.'

The man thanked me, calling down blessings on me, and as we talked the other traders, each of whom had thrown down a carcass, heard the sound of our voices and came up to us. They congratulated me on my escape and, when they had taken me away with them, I told them my whole story, explaining the perils that I had endured on my voyage as well as the reason why I had got to the valley. After that, I presented many of the diamonds that I had with me to the man who had thrown down the carcass that I had used, and in his delight he renewed his blessings. The others exclaimed: 'By God, fate has granted you a second life, for you are the first man ever to come here and escape from the valley. God be praised that you are safe.'

I passed the night with them in a spot that was both pleasant and safe, delighted that I had escaped unhurt from the valley of the snakes and had got back to inhabited parts. At dawn we got up, and as we moved across the great mountain we could see huge numbers of snakes in the valley, but we kept on our way until we reached an orchard on a large and beautiful island, where there were camphor trees, each one of which could provide shade for a hundred people. Whoever wants to get some camphor must use a long tool to bore a hole at the top of the tree and then collect what comes out. The liquid camphor flows down and then solidifies like gum, as this is the sap of the tree, and when it dries up, it can be used for firewood. On the island is a type of wild beast known as the rhinoceros, which grazes there just as cows and buffaloes do in our own parts. It is a huge beast with a body larger than that of a camel, a herbivore with a single horn some ten cubits long in the centre of its head containing what looks like the image of a man. There is also a species of cattle there. According to seafarers and travellers who have visited the mountain and its districts there, this rhinoceros can carry a large elephant on its horn and go on pasturing in the island and on the shore without paying any attention to it. The elephant, impaled on its horn, will then die, and in the heat of the sun grease from its corpse will trickle on to the head of the rhinoceros. When this gets into its eyes, it will go blind, and as it then lies down by the coast, a *rukh* will swoop on it and carry it off in its talons in order to feed its chicks both with the beast itself and with what is on its horn. On the island I saw many buffaloes of a type unlike any that we have at home.

I exchanged a number of the stones that I had brought with me in my pocket from the diamond valley with the traders in return for a cash payment and some of the goods that they had brought with them, which they carried for me. I travelled on in their company, inspecting different lands and God's creations, from one valley and one city to another, buying and selling as we went, until we arrived at Basra. We stayed there for a few days and then I returned to Baghdad.

When Sindbad reached Baghdad, the City of Peace, he went to his own district and entered his house. He had with him a large number of diamonds, as well as cash and a splendid display of all kinds of goods. After he had met his family and his relatives, he dispensed alms and gave gifts to every one of his relations and companions. He began to enjoy good food and wine, to dress in fine clothes and to frequent the company of his friends. He forgot all his past sufferings, and he continued to enjoy a pleasant, relaxed and contented life, with entertainments of all sorts. All those who had heard of his return would come and ask him about his voyage and about the lands that he had visited. He would tell them of his experiences and amaze them by recounting the difficulties with which he had to contend, after which they would congratulate him on his safe return.

When he had told all this to Sindbad the landsman, those present were filled with astonishment. They all dined with him that evening and he gave orders that the second Sindbad be given a hundred *mithqals* of gold. Sindbad the landsman took these and went on his way, marvelling at what his host had endured, and, filled with gratitude, when he reached his own house, he called down blessings on him.

The next morning, when it was light, he got up and, having performed the morning prayer, he went back to the house of Sindbad the sailor as he had been told to do. On his arrival he said good morning to his host, who welcomed him, and the two sat together until the rest of the company arrived. When they had eaten and drunk and were pleasantly and cheerfully relaxed, SINDBAD THE SAILOR SAID:

The Black Giant

Listen with attention to this tale of mine, my brothers, for it is more wonderful than what I told you before, and it is God Whose knowledge and decree regulate the unknown. When I got back from my voyage I was happy, relaxed and glad to be safe, and, as I told you yesterday, I had made a large amount of money, since God had replaced for me all that I had lost. So I stayed in Baghdad for a time, enjoying my good fortune with happiness and contentment, but then I began to feel an urge to travel again and to see the world, as well as to make a profit by trading, for as the proverb says: 'The soul instructs us to do evil.' After thinking the matter over, I bought a large quantity of goods suitable for a trading voyage, packed them up and took them from Baghdad to Basra. I went to the shore, where I saw a large ship on which were many virtuous merchants and passengers, as well as a pious crew of devout and godly sailors. I embarked with them and we set sail with the blessing of Almighty God and His beneficent aid, confident of success and safety.

On we sailed from sea to sea, island to island and city to city, enjoying the sights that we saw, and happy with our trading, until one day, when we were in the middle of a boisterous sea with buffeting waves, the captain, who was keeping a lookout from the gunwale, gave a great cry, slapped his face, plucked at his beard and tore his clothes. He ordered the sails to be furled and the anchors dropped. 'What is it, captain?' we asked him, and he told us to pray for safety, explaining: 'The wind got the better of us, forcing us out to sea, and ill fortune has driven us to the mountain of the hairy ones, an ape-like folk. No one who has come there has ever escaped, and I feel in my heart that we shall all die.' Before he had finished speaking we were surrounded on all sides by apes who were like a flock of locusts, approaching our ship and spreading out on the shore. We were afraid to kill any of them or to strike them and drive them off, as we thought that if we did, they would be certain to kill us because of their numbers, since 'numbers defeat courage', as the proverb has it. We could only wait in fear lest they plunder our stores and our goods.

These apes are the ugliest of creatures, with hair like black felt and a horrifying appearance; no one can understand anything they say and they have an aversion to men. They have yellow eyes and black faccs and are small, each being four spans in height. They climbed on to the anchor cables and gnawed through them with their teeth before proceeding to cut all the other ropes throughout the ship. As we could not keep head to wind, the ship came to rest by the mountain of the ape men and grounded there. The apes seized all the merchants and the others, bringing them to shore, after which they took the ship and everything in it, carrying off their spoils and going on their way. We were left on the island, unable to see the ship and without any idea where they had taken it.

We stayed there eating fruits and herbs and drinking from the streams until we caught sight of some form of habitation in the centre of the island. We walked towards this and found that it was a strongly built castle with high walls and an ebony gate whose twin leaves were standing open. We went through the gate and discovered a wide space like an extensive courtyard around which were a number of lofty doors, while at the top of it was a large and high stone bench. Cooking pots hung there on stoves surrounded by great quantities of bones, but there was nobody to be seen. We were astonished by all this and we sat down there for a while, after which we fell asleep and stayed sleeping from the forenoon until sunset. It was then that the earth shook beneath us, there was a thunderous sound, and from the top of the castle down came an enormous creature shaped like a man, black, tall as a lofty palm tree, with eyes like sparks of fire. He had tusks like those of a boar, a huge mouth like the top of a well, lips like those of a camel, which hung down over his chest, ears like large boats resting on his shoulders, and fingernails like the claws of a lion. When we saw what he looked like, we were so terrified that we almost lost our senses and were half-dead from fear and terror.

When he had reached the ground, he sat for a short while on the bench before getting up and coming over to us. He singled me out from among the other traders who were with me, grasping my hand and lifting me from the ground. Then he felt me and turned me over, but in his hands I was no more than a small mouthful, and when he had examined me as a butcher examines a sheep for slaughter, he found that I had been weakened by my sufferings and emaciated by the discomforts of the voyage, which had left me skinny. So he let go of me and picked another of my companions in my place. After turning him over and feeling him as he had felt me, he let him go too and he kept on doing this with us, one after the other, until he came to the captain, a powerful man, stout and thickset with broad shoulders. He was pleased with what he had found and, after laying hold of the man as a butcher holds his victim, he threw him down on the ground and set his foot on his neck, which he broke. Then he took a long spit, which he thrust up from the captain's backside to the crown of his head, after which the creature lit a large fire and over this he placed the spit on which the captain was skewered. He turned this round and round over the coals until, when the flesh was cooked, he took it off the fire, put it down in front of him and dismembered it, as a man dismembers a chicken. He started to tear the flesh with his fingernails and then to eat it. When he had finished it all, he gnawed the bones, leaving none of them untouched, before throwing away what was left of them at the side of the castle. He then sat for a while before stretching himself out on the bench and falling asleep, snorting like a sheep or a beast with its throat cut. He slept until morning and then got up and went off about his business.

When we were sure that he had gone we began to talk to one another, weeping over our plight and exclaiming: 'Would that we had been drowned or eaten by the ape men, for this would have been better than being roasted over the coals! That is a terrible death, but God's will be done, for there is no might and no power except with Him, the Exalted, the Omnipotent. We shall die miserably without anyone knowing about us, as there is no way left to us to escape from this place.' Then we went off into the island to look for a hiding place or a means of escape, as we didn't mind dying provided we were not roasted over the fire. But we found nowhere to hide and when evening came we were so afraid that we went back to the castle.

We had only been sitting there for a short while before the ground beneath us began to shake again and the black giant came up to us. He started turning us over and inspecting us one by one as he had done the first time, until he found one to his liking. He seized this man and treated him as he had treated the captain the day before, roasting and eating him. He then went to sleep on the bench and slept the night through, snorting like a slaughtered beast. When day broke he got up and went away, leaving us, as he had done before. We gathered together to talk, telling one another: 'By God, it would be better to throw ourselves into the sea and drown rather than be roasted, for that is an abominable death.' At that point one of our number said: 'Listen to me. We must find some way of killing the giant so as to free ourselves from the distress that he has caused us, and also to free our fellow Muslims from his hostility and tyranny.' I said: 'Brothers, listen. If we have to kill him, we must move some of these timbers and this wood and make ourselves a species of ship. If we then think of a way of killing him, we can embark on it and put out to sea, going wherever God wills, or else we could stay here until a ship sails by on which we might take passage. If we fail to kill him, we can come down and put out to sea, for even if we drown we would still escape being slaughtered and roasted over the fire. If we escape, we escape, and if we drown, we die as martyrs.' 'This is sound advice,' they all agreed, and we then set to work moving timbers out of the castle and building a boat which we moored by the shore, loading it with some provisions. Afterwards we went back to the castle.

When evening came, the earth shook and the black giant arrived like a ravening dog. He turned us over and felt us one by one before picking out one of us, whom he treated as he had done the others. Having eaten him he fell asleep on the bench, with thunderous snorts. We got up and took two iron spits from those that were standing there. We put them in the fierce fire until they were red hot, like burning coals, and then, gripping them firmly, we carried them to the sleeping, snoring giant, placed them on his eyes and then bore down on them with our combined strength as firmly as we could. The spits entered his eyes and blinded him, at which he terrified us by uttering a great cry. He sprang up from the bench and began to hunt for us as we fled right and left. In his blinded state he could not see us, but we were still terrified of him, thinking that our last hour had come and despairing of escape. He felt his way to the door and went out bellowing, leaving us quaking with fear as the earth shook beneath our feet because of the violence of his cries. We followed him out as he went off in search of us, but then he came back with two others, larger and more ferocious-looking than himself. When we saw him and his even more hideous companions, we panicked, and as they caught sight of us and hurried towards us, we boarded our boat, cast off its moorings and drove it out to sea. Each of the giants had a huge rock in his hands, which they threw at us, killing most of us and leaving only me and two others.

The boat took us to another island and there we walked until nightfall, when, in our wretched state, we fell asleep for a little while, but when we woke, it was only to see that a huge snake with an enormous body and a wide belly had coiled around us. It made for one of us and swallowed his body as far as the shoulders, after which it gulped down the rest of him and we could hear his ribs cracking in its belly. Then it went off, leaving us astonished, filled with grief for our companion and fearful for our own safety. We exclaimed: 'By God, it is amazing that each death should be more hideous than the one before! We were glad to have got away from the black giant but our joy has been short-lived, and there is no might and no power except with God. By God, we managed to escape from the giant and from death by drowning, but how are we to escape from this sinister monster?'

We walked around the island until evening, eating its fruits and drinking from its streams, until we discovered a huge and lofty tree which we climbed in order to sleep there. I was up on the top-most branch, and when night fell the snake came through the darkness and, having looked right and left, it made for our tree and swarmed up until it had reached my companion. It swallowed his body as far as the shoulders, and then coiled round the tree with him until I heard his bones cracking in its belly, after which it swallowed the rest of him before my eyes. It then slid down the tree and went away. I stayed on my branch for the rest of the night and when daylight came, I climbed down again, half-dead with fear and terror. I thought of throwing myself into the sea to find rest from the troubles of the world, but I could not bring myself to commit suicide, as life is dear. So I fastened a broad wooden beam across my feet with two other similar beams on my right and my left sides, another over my stomach, and a very large one laterally over my head, to match the one beneath my feet. I was in the middle of these beams, which encased me on all sides, and after I had fastened them securely, I threw myself, with all of them, on to the ground. I lay between them as though I was in a cupboard, and when night fell and the snake arrived as usual, it saw me and made for me but could not swallow me up as I was protected on all sides by the beams and, although it circled round, it could find no way to reach me. I watched it, nearly dead with fear, as it went off and then came back, constantly trying to get to me in order to swallow me, but the beams that I had fastened all around me prevented it. This continued from sunset until dawn, and when the sun rose the snake went off, frustrated and angry, and I then stretched out my hand and freed myself from the beams, still half-dead because of the terror that it had inflicted on me.

After I had got up, I walked to the end of the island, and when I looked out from the shore, there far out at sea was a ship. I took a large branch and waved it in its direction, calling out to the sailors. They saw me and told each other: 'We must look to see what this is, as it might be a man.' When they had sailed near enough to hear my shouts, they came in and brought me on board. They asked for my story, and I told them everything that had happened to me from beginning to end, and they were amazed at the hardships I had endured. They gave me some of their own clothes to hide my nakedness and then brought me some food, allowing me to eat my fill, as well as providing me with cold, fresh water. This revived and refreshed me, and such was my relief that it was as though God had brought me back from the dead. I praised and thanked Him for His abundant grace, and although I had been sure that I was doomed, I regained my composure to such an extent that it seemed as if all my perils had been a dream.

My rescuers sailed on with a fair wind granted by Almighty God until we came in sight of an island called al-Salahita, where the captain dropped anchor. Everyone disembarked, merchants and passengers alike, unloading their wares in order to trade. The master of the ship then turned to me and said: 'Listen to me. You are a poor stranger who has gone through a terrifying ordeal, as you have told us, and so I want to do something for you that may help you get back to your own land and cause you to bless me for the rest of your life.' When I had thanked him for this he went on to say: 'We lost one of our passengers, and we don't know whether he is alive or dead, as we have heard no news of him. I propose to hand over his goods to you so that you may sell them here in return for payment that we shall give you for your trouble. Anything left over we shall keep until we get back to

Baghdad, where we can make enquiries about his family, and we shall then hand over the rest of the goods to them, as well as the price of what has been sold. Are you prepared to take charge of these things, land them on the island and trade with them?' 'To hear is to obey, sir,' I said, adding my blessings and thanks for his generous conduct. So he ordered the porters and members of the crew to unload the goods on the shore and then to hand them over to me. The ship's clerk asked him whose goods these were so that he could enter the name of the merchant who owned them. 'Write on them the name of Sindbad the sailor,' the master told him, 'the man who came out with us but was lost on an island. We never heard of him again, and I want this stranger to sell them and give us what they fetch in return for a fee for his trouble in selling them. Whatever is unsold we can take back to Baghdad, and if we find Sindbad, we can give it back to him, but if not, we can hand it over to his family in the city.' 'Well said!' exclaimed the clerk. 'That is a good plan.'

When I heard the master say that the bales were to be entered under my name, I told myself: 'By God, I am Sindbad the sailor, who was one of those lost on the island,' but I waited in patience until the merchants had left the ship and were all there together talking about trade. It was then that I went up to the master and said: 'Sir, do you know anything about the owner of these bales that you have entrusted to me to sell for him?' 'I know nothing about his circumstances,' the master replied, 'only that he was a Baghdadi called Sindbad the sailor. We anchored off an island, where a large number of our people were lost in the sea, including Sindbad, and until this day we have heard nothing more about him.' At that I gave a great cry and said: 'Master, may God keep you safe. Know that I am Sindbad the sailor and that I was not drowned. When you anchored there, I landed with the other merchants and passengers and went off to a corner of the island, taking some food with me. I so enjoyed sitting there that I became drowsy and fell into the soundest of sleeps, and when I woke up I found the ship gone and no one else there with me. So these are my belongings and my goods. All the merchants who fetch diamonds saw me when I was on the diamond mountain and they will confirm that I am, in fact, Sindbad. For I told them the story of what had happened to me on your ship and how you forgot about me and left me lying asleep on the island and what happened to me after I woke up and found no one there.'

When the merchants and the passengers heard what I had to say, they gathered around me, some believing me and some convinced that I was lying. While things were still undecided, one of the merchants who heard me mention the diamond valley got up and came to me. He asked the company to listen to him and said: 'I told you of the most remarkable thing that I saw on my travels, which happened when my companions and I were throwing down carcasses into the diamond valley. I threw mine down as usual and when it was brought up by an eagle there was a man attached to it. You didn't believe me and thought that I was lying.' 'Yes,' said the others, 'you certainly told us this and we didn't believe you.' 'Here is the man who was clinging to it,' said the merchant. 'He presented me with valuable diamonds whose like is nowhere to be found, giving me more than I had ever got from a carcass, and he then stayed with me until we reached Basra, after which he went off to his own city. My companions and I said goodbye to him and went back to our own lands. This is the man. He told us that his name was Sindbad the sailor and that his ship had gone off leaving him on the island. He has come here as proof to you that I was telling the truth. All these goods are his; he told us about them when we met and what he has said has been shown to be true.'

When the master heard this he came up to me and looked carefully at me for some time. Then he asked: 'What mark is on your goods?' I told him what it was and then I mentioned some dealings that we had had together on our voyage from Basra. He was then convinced that I really was Sindbad and embraced me, saluting me and congratulating me on my safe return. 'By God, sir,' he said, 'yours is a remarkable story and a strange affair. Praise be to God, Who has reunited us and returned your goods and possessions to you.' After that I used my expertise to dispose of my goods, making a great profit on the trip. I was delighted by this, congratulating myself on my safety and on the return of my possessions.

We continued to trade among the islands until we came to Sind, where we bought and sold, and in the sea there I came across innumerable wonders. Among them was a fish that looked like a cow and another resembling a donkey, together with a bird that came out of a mollusc shell, laying its eggs and rearing its chicks on the surface of the sea and never coming out on to dry land at all. On we sailed, with the permission of Almighty God, enjoying a fair wind and a pleasant voyage until we got back to Basra. I stayed there for a few days before going to Baghdad, where I went to my own district and entered my house, greeting my family as well as my friends and companions. Feeling joyful at my safe return to my country, my family, my city and my properties, I distributed alms, made gifts, clothed widows and orphans and gathered together my companions and friends. I went on like this, eating, drinking and enjoying myself with good food, good wine and friends, having made a vast profit from my voyage and having forgotten all that had happened to me and the hardships and terrors that I had endured.

Sindbad the sailor then gave orders that Sindbad the porter should be given his usual hundred *mithqals* of gold and that tables should be laid with food. The whole company ate with him, still filled with amazement at the tale of their host's experiences, and then after supper they went on their ways. As for Sindbad the porter, he took his gold and went off astonished by what he had heard. He spent the night at home and the next morning, when it was light, he got up, performed the morning prayer and walked to the house of Sindbad the sailor, greeting him as he went in. His host welcomed him with gladness and delight, making him sit with him until the rest of his companions arrived. Food was produced and they ate, drank and enjoyed themselves, until SINDBAD BEGAN TO SPEAK:

The Cannibal King

Know, my brothers, that when I got back to Baghdad and met my companions, my family and my friends I enjoyed a life of the greatest happiness, contentment and relaxation, forgetting everything in my well-being, and drowning in pleasure and delight in the company of my friends and companions. It was while my life was at its most pleasant that I felt a pernicious urge to travel to foreign parts, to associate with different races and to trade and make a profit. Having thought this over, I bought more valuable goods, suitable for a voyage, than I had ever taken before, packing them into bales. When I had gone down from Baghdad to Basra I loaded them on a ship, taking with me a number of the leading Basran merchants. We put out, with the blessing of Almighty God, on to the turbulent and boisterous sea and for a number of nights and days we had a good voyage, passing from island to island and sea to sea until one day we met a contrary wind. The master used the anchors to bring us to a halt in mid-ocean lest we founder there, but while we were addressing our supplications to Almighty God a violent gale blew up, which tore our sails to shreds, plunging all on board into the sea, together with all their bales, goods and belongings.

I was with the others in the sea. I swam for half a day, but I had given up all hope when Almighty God sent me part of one of the ship's timbers on to which I climbed, together with some of the other merchants. We huddled together as we rode on it, paddling with our legs, and being helped by the waves and the wind. This went on for a day and a night, but in the forenoon of the second day the wind rose and the sea became stormy, with powerful waves. The current then cast us up on an island, half-dead through lack of sleep, fatigue and cold, hunger, thirst and fear. Later, when we walked around the place, we found many plants, some of which we ate to allay our hunger and sustain us, and we spent the night by the shore. The next day, when it was light, we got up and continued to explore the various parts of the island. In the distance we caught sight of a building and kept on walking towards it until we stood at its door. While we were there, out came a crowd of naked men, who took hold of us without a word and brought us to their king. We sat down at his command and food was brought which we did not recognize and whose like we had never seen in our lives. I could not bring myself to take it and so I ate nothing, unlike my companions, and this abstemiousness on my part was thanks to the grace of Almighty God as it was this that has allowed me to live until now.

When my companions tasted the food, their wits went wandering; they fell on it like madmen and were no longer the same men. The king's servants then fetched them coconut oil, some of which was poured out as drink and some of which was smeared over them. When my companions drank the oil their eyes swivelled in their heads and they started to eat the food in an unnatural way. I felt sorry for them, but I did not know what to do about it and I was filled with great uneasiness, fearing for my own life at the hands of the naked men. For when I looked at them closely I could see that they were Magians and that the king of their city was a *ghul*. They would bring him everyone who came to their country or whom they saw or met in their valley or its roads. The newcomer would then be given that food and anointed with that oil;

his belly would swell so that he could eat more and more; he would lose his mind and his powers of thought until he became like an imbecile. The Magians would continue to stuff him with food and coconut oil drink until, when he was fat enough, they would cut his throat and feed him to the king. They themselves would eat human flesh unroasted and raw.

When I saw this I was filled with distress both for myself and for my comrades, who, in their bewildered state, did not realize what was being done to them. They were put in the charge of a man who would herd them around the island like cattle; as for me, fear and hunger made me weak and sickly, and my flesh clung to my bones. The Magians, seeing my condition, left me alone and forgot about me. Not one of them remembered me or thought about me, and so one day I contrived to move from the place where they were, and walked away, leaving it far behind me. I then saw a herdsman sitting on a high promontory, and when I looked more closely I could see that he was the man who had been given the job of pasturing not only my companions but many others as well, who were in the same state. When he saw me he realized that I was still in possession of my wits and was not suffering from what had affected the others. So he gestured to me from far off, indicating that I should turn back and then take the road to the right, which would lead to the main highway. I followed his instructions and went back, and when I saw a road on my right I followed it, at times running in terror and then walking more slowly until I was rested. I went on like this until I was out of sight of the man who had shown me the way and I could no longer see him nor could he see me.

The sun then set and as darkness fell I sat down to rest, intending to go to sleep, but I was too afraid, too hungry and too tired to sleep that night. At midnight I got up and walked further into the island, carrying on until daybreak, when the sun rose over the hilltops and the valleys. I was exhausted, hungry and thirsty and so I started to eat grass and some of the island plants, going on until I had satisfied my hunger and was satiated. Then I got up and walked on, and I continued like this for the whole of the day and the night, eating plants whenever I was hungry. This went on for seven days and seven nights until, on the morning of the eighth day, I caught sight of something in the distance and set off towards it. I got to my destination after sunset and looked carefully at it from far off, as my heart was still fluttering because of my earlier sufferings, but it turned out to be a group of men gathering peppercorns. They saw me as I approached and quickly came and surrounded me on all sides, asking me who I was and where I had come from. I told them that I was a poor unfortunate and then went on to give them my whole story, explaining my perils, hardships and sufferings.

'By God,' they exclaimed, 'this is an amazing story, but how did you escape from the blacks and get away from them on the island? There are vast numbers of them and as they are cannibals no one can pass them in safety.' So I told them what had happened to me and how they had taken my companions by feeding them on some food which I did not eat. They were astonished by my experiences and, after congratulating me on my safety, they made me sit with them until they had finished their work, after which they brought me some tasty food, which I ate because I was starving. I stayed with them for some time and then they took me with them on a ship, which brought me to the island where they lived. There they presented me to their king, whom I greeted and who welcomed me courteously and asked me about myself. I told him of my circumstances and of all my experiences from the day that I left Baghdad until I came to him. He and those with him were filled with astonishment at this tale. He told me to sit by him and he then ordered food to be brought, from which I ate my fill. Then I washed my hands and thanked, praised and extolled Almighty God for His grace.

When I left the king's court I looked around the city, which was a thriving place, populous and wealthy, well stocked with provisions and full of markets and trade goods, as well as with both buyers and sellers. I was pleased and happy to have got there, and I made friends with the people, and their king, who treated me with more honour and respect than he showed to his own leading citizens. I observed that all of them, high and low alike, rode good horses but without saddles. I was surprised at that and I asked the king why it was, pointing out that a saddle made things more comfortable for the rider and allowed him to exert more force. 'What is a saddle?' he asked, adding: 'I have never seen one or ridden on one in my life.' 'Would you allow me to make you one so that you could ride on it and see its advantages?' I asked, and when he told me to carry on, I asked him to provide me with some wood. He ordered everything I needed to be fetched, after which I looked for a clever carpenter and sat teaching him how saddles should be made. Then I got wool, carded it and made it into felt, after which I covered the saddle in leather and polished it before attaching bands and fastening the girth. Next I fetched a smith and explained to him how to make stirrups. When he had made a large pair, I filed them down and then covered them with tin, giving them fringes of silk. I fetched one of the best of the king's horses, a stallion, which I then saddled and bridled, and when I had attached the stirrups I brought him to the king. What I had done took the fancy of the king, who was filled with admiration, and, having thanked me, he mounted the horse and was delighted by the saddle. In return for my work he gave me a huge reward, and when his vizier saw what I had made, he asked for another saddle like it. I made him one and after that all the principal officers of state and the state officials began to ask me to make them saddles. I taught the carpenter how to produce them and showed the smith how to make stirrups, after which we started to manufacture them and to sell them to great men and the employers of labour. This brought me a great deal of money and I became a man of importance in the city, commanding ever greater affection and enjoying high status both with the king and with his court, and also with the leading citizens and state officials.

One day, while I was sitting with the king enjoying my dignity to the full, he said to me: 'You have become a respected and honoured companion of ours; you are one of us and we cannot bear to be parted from you or that you should leave our city. I have something to ask of you, and I want you to obey me and not to reject my request.' 'What is it that you want of me, your majesty?' I asked, adding: 'I cannot refuse you, because you have treated me with such kindness, favour and generosity, and I thank God that I have become one of your servants.' The king said: 'I want you to take a wife here, a beautiful, graceful and witty lady, as wealthy as she is lovely, so that you may become one of our citizens and I can lodge you with me in my palace. Do not disobey me or reject my proposal.' When I heard what he said, I was too embarrassed to speak and stayed silent. Then, when he asked why I did not answer, I said: 'My master, king of the age, your commands must be obeyed.' He sent at once for the *qadi* and the notaries, and he married me on the spot to a noble lady of high birth and great wealth, who combined beauty and grace with her distinguished ancestry, and who was the owner of houses, properties and estates.

After the king had married me to the great lady,

he presented me with a fine, large detached house, providing me with eunuchs and retainers and assigning me pay and allowances. I lived a life of ease, happy and relaxed, forgetting all the toils, difficulties and hardships that I had experienced. I told myself that when I went back to my own country, I would take my wife with me, but there is no avoiding fate and no one knows what will happen to him. My wife and I were deeply in love; we lived in harmony, enjoying a life of pleasure and plenty over a period of time. Almighty God then widowed a neighbour of mine, and, as he was a friend of mine, I went to his house to offer my condolences on his loss. I found him in the worst of states, full of care and sick at heart. I tried to console him by saying: 'Don't grieve for your wife. Almighty God will see that you are well recompensed by providing you with another, more beautiful one, and, if it is His will, you will live a long life.' He wept bitterly and said: 'My friend, how can I marry another wife and how can God compensate me with a better one when I have only one day left to live?' 'Come back to your senses, brother,' I told him, 'and don't forecast your own death, for you are sound and healthy.' 'My friend,' he said, 'I swear by your life that tomorrow you will lose me and never see me again.' 'How can that be?' I asked him, and he told me: 'Today my wife will be buried and I shall be buried with her in the same grave. It is the custom here that, when a wife dies, her husband is buried alive with her, while if the husband dies it is the wife who suffers this fate, so that neither partner may enjoy life after the death of the other.' 'By God,' I exclaimed, 'what a dreadful custom! This is unbearable!'

While we were talking, a group comprising the bulk of the citizens of the town arrived and started to pay condolences to my friend on the loss of his wife and on his own fate. They began to lay out the corpse in their usual way, fetching a coffin in which they carried it, accompanied by the husband. They took it out of the city to a place on the side of a mountain overlooking the sea. When they got there, they lifted up a huge stone, under which could be seen a rocky cleft like the shaft of a well.

They threw the woman's body down this, into what I could see was a great underground pit. Then they brought my friend, tied a rope round his waist and lowered him into the pit, providing him with a large jug of fresh water and seven loaves by way of provisions. When he had been lowered down, he freed himself from the rope, which they pulled up before putting the stone back in its place and going away, leaving my friend with his wife in the pit.

I said to myself: 'By God, this death is even more frightful than the previous one,' and I went to the king and asked him how it was that in his country they buried the living with the dead. He said: 'This is our custom here. When the husband dies we bury his wife with him, and when the wife dies we bury her husband alive so that they may not be parted either in life or in death. This is a tradition handed down from our ancestors.' I asked him: 'O king of the age, in the case of a foreigner like me, if his wife dies here, would you treat him as you treated my friend?' 'Yes,' he replied, 'we would bury him with her just as you have seen.'

When I heard this, I was so concerned and distressed for myself that my gall bladder almost split and in my dismay I began to fear that my wife might die before me and that I would be buried alive with her. Then I tried to console myself, telling myself that it might be I who died first, for no one knows who will be first and who second. I tried to amuse myself in various ways, but within a short time my wife fell ill and a few days later she was dead. Most of the townsfolk came to pay their condolences to me and her family, and among those who came in accordance with their custom was the king. They fetched professionals who washed her corpse and dressed her in the most splendid of her clothes together with the best of her jewellery, necklaces and precious gems before placing her in her coffin. They then carried her off to the mountain, removed the stone from the mouth of the pit and threw her into it. My friends and my wife's family came up to take a last farewell of me. I was calling out: 'I'm a foreigner! I don't have to put up with your customs,' but they did not listen or pay any attention to me. Instead they seized me and used force to tie me up, attaching the seven loaves and the jug of fresh water that their custom required, before lowering me into the pit, which turned out to be a vast cavern under the mountain. 'Loose yourself from the rope!' they shouted, but I wasn't willing to do that and so they threw the rest of it down on top of me before replacing the huge stone that covered the entrance and going away.

In the pit I came across very many corpses together with a foul stink of putrefaction and I blamed myself for my own actions, telling myself that I deserved everything that had happened to me. While I was there I could not distinguish night from day and I began by putting myself on short rations, not eating until I was half-dead with hunger and drinking only when I was violently thirsty, because I was afraid of exhausting my food and my water. I recited the formula: 'There is no might and no power except with God, the Exalted, the Omnipotent,' adding: 'Why did I have the misfortune to marry in this city? Every time I say to myself that I have escaped from one disaster, I fall into another that is worse. By God, this is a terrible death. I wish that I had been drowned at sea or had died on the mountains, for that would have been better than this miserable end.'

I went on like this, blaming myself, sleeping on the bones of the dead and calling on Almighty God to aid me. I longed for death, but, in spite of my plight, death would not come and this continued until I was consumed by hunger and parched by thirst. I sat down and felt for my bread, after which I ate a little and drank a little before getting up and walking round the cavern. This was wide with some empty hollows, but the surface was covered with bodies as well as old dry bones. I made a place for myself at the side of it, far away from the recent corpses, and there I slept. I now had very little food left and I would only take one mouthful and one sip of water each day or at even longer intervals for fear of using up both food and water before my death. Things went on like this until one day, as I was sitting thinking about what I would do when my provisions were exhausted, the stone was suddenly moved and light shone down on me. While I was wondering what was happening, I saw people standing at the head of the shaft. They lowered a dead man and a live woman, who was weeping and screaming, and with her they sent down a large quantity of food and water. I watched her but she didn't see me, and when the stone had been replaced and the people had gone, I stood up with the shin bone of a dead man in my hand and, going up to her, I struck her on the middle of her head. She fell unconscious on the ground and I struck her a second and a third time, so killing her. I took her bread and what else she had, for I noticed she had with her a large quantity of ornaments, robes, necklaces, jewels and precious stones. When I had removed her food and water, I sat down to sleep in my place by the side of the cavern. Later I began to eat as little of the food as was needed to keep me alive lest it be used up too soon, leaving me to die of hunger and thirst.

I stayed down there for some time, killing all those who were buried alive with the dead and taking their food and water in order to survive. Then, one day, I woke from sleep to hear something making a noise at the side of the cavern. I asked myself what it could be, and so I got up and went towards whatever it was, carrying with me a dead man's shin bone. When the thing that was making the noise heard me, it fled away and I could see that it was an animal. I followed it to the upper part of the cave and there coming through a little hole I could see a ray of light like a star, appearing and then disappearing. At the sight of this, I made my way towards it, and the nearer I got, the broader the beam of light became, leaving me certain that there was an opening in the cave leading to the outer world. 'There must be some reason for this,' I said to myself. 'Either it is another opening, like the one through which I was lowered, or it is crack leading out of here.' I thought the matter over for a while and then went towards the light. Here I discovered that there was a tunnel dug by wild beasts from the surface of the mountain to allow them to get in, eat their fill of the corpses and then get out again. On seeing this I calmed down, regained my composure and relaxed, being certain that, after my brush with death, I would manage to stay alive.

Like a man in a dream, I struggled through the tunnel to find myself overlooking the sea coast on a high and impassable mountain promontory that cut off the island and its city from the seas that met there. In my delight, I gave praise and thanks to God, and then, taking heart, I went back through the tunnel to the cave and removed all the food and water that I had saved. I took some clothes from the dead to put on in place of my own, and I also collected a quantity of what they were wearing in the way of necklaces, gems, strings of pearls and jewellery of silver and gold, studded with precious stones of all kinds, together with other rare items. I fastened the clothes of the dead to my own and went through the tunnel to stand by the seashore. Every day I would go back down to inspect the cave, and whenever there was a burial I would kill the survivor, whether it was a man or a woman, and take the food and the water. Then I would go out of the tunnel and sit by the shore, waiting for Almighty God to send me relief in the form of a passing ship. I started to remove all the jewellery that I could see from the cave, tying it up in dead men's clothes.

Things went on like this for some time until one day, while I was sitting by the shore, I saw a passing ship out at sea in the middle of the waves. I took something white from the clothes of the dead, fastened it to a stick and ran along with it, parallel to the shore, waving it towards the ship, until the crew turned and caught sight of me as I stood on a high point. They put in towards me until they could hear my voice, and then they sent me a boat manned by some of their crew. As they came close they said: 'Who are you and why are you sitting there? How did you get to this mountain? Never in our lives have we seen anyone who managed to reach it.' I told them: 'I'm a merchant whose ship was sunk. I got on a plank together with my belongings, and by God's aid I was able to come up on shore here, bringing them with me, but only after I had exerted myself and used all my skill in a hard struggle.'

The sailors took me with them in the boat, carrying what I had fetched from the cave tied up in clothes and shrouds. They brought me to the ship, together with all of these things, and took me to the master, who asked: 'Man, how did you get here? This is a huge mountain with a great city on the other side of it, but although I have spent my life sailing this sea and passing by it, I have never seen anything on it except beasts and birds.' 'I'm a merchant,' I told him, 'but the large ship on which I was sailing broke up and sank. All these goods of mine, and the clothes that you see, were plunged into the water, but I managed to load them on to a large beam from the ship and fate helped me to come to shore by this mountain, after which I waited for someone to pass by and take me off.' I said nothing about what had happened to me in the city or in the cave, for fear that someone on board might be from the city. Then I took a quantity of my goods to the master of the ship and said: 'Sir, it is thanks to you that I have escaped from this mountain, so please take these things in return for the kindness you have shown me.' The master did not accept, insisting: 'We take no gifts from anyone, and if we see a shipwrecked man on the coast or on an island we take him with us and give him food and water. If he is naked we clothe him, and when we reach a safe haven we give him a present from what we have with us as an act of generosity for the sake of Almighty God.' On hearing that, I prayed God to grant him a long life.

We then sailed on from island to island and from sea to sea. I was hopeful that I would escape my difficulties, but although I was full of joy that I had been saved, whenever I thought of how I had sat in the cave with my wife I would almost go out of my mind. Through the power of God we came safely to Basra, where I landed and spent a few days before going on to Baghdad. There I went to my own district and, when I had entered my house, I met my family and friends and asked them how they were. They were delighted by my safe return and congratulated me. I then stored all the goods that I had with me in my warehouses and distributed alms and gifts, providing clothes for the widows and orphans. I was filled with joy and delight and renewed old ties with friends and companions, enjoying amusements and entertainments.

These, then, were the most remarkable things that happened to me on my fourth voyage, but, my brother, dine with me this evening, take your usual present of gold, come back tomorrow and I shall tell you of my experiences on my fifth voyage, as these were stranger and more wonderful than anything that happened before.

Sindbad the sailor then ordered that Sindbad the porter be given a hundred *mithqals* of gold. Tables were set and the company dined, before dispersing in a state of astonishment, as each story was more surprising than the last. Sindbad the porter went home and spent the night filled with happiness and contentedness as well as with amazement.

1. BOCCACCIO · *Mrs Rosie and the Priest*
2. GERARD MANLEY HOPKINS · *As kingfishers catch fire*
3. *The Saga of Gunnlaug Serpent-tongue*
4. THOMAS DE QUINCEY · *On Murder Considered as One of the Fine Arts*
5. FRIEDRICH NIETZSCHE · *Aphorisms on Love and Hate*
6. JOHN RUSKIN · *Traffic*
7. PU SONGLING · *Wailing Ghosts*
8. JONATHAN SWIFT · *A Modest Proposal*
9. *Three Tang Dynasty Poets*
10. WALT WHITMAN · *On the Beach at Night Alone*
11. KENKŌ · *A Cup of Sake Beneath the Cherry Trees*
12. BALTASAR GRACIÁN · *How to Use Your Enemies*
13. JOHN KEATS · *The Eve of St Agnes*
14. THOMAS HARDY · *Woman much missed*
15. GUY DE MAUPASSANT · *Femme Fatale*
16. MARCO POLO · *Travels in the Land of Serpents and Pearls*
17. SUETONIUS · *Caligula*
18. APOLLONIUS OF RHODES · *Jason and Medea*
19. ROBERT LOUIS STEVENSON · *Olalla*
20. KARL MARX AND FRIEDRICH ENGELS · *The Communist Manifesto*
21. PETRONIUS · *Trimalchio's Feast*
22. JOHANN PETER HEBEL · *How a Ghastly Story Was Brought to Light by a Common or Garden Butcher's Dog*
23. HANS CHRISTIAN ANDERSEN · *The Tinder Box*
24. RUDYARD KIPLING · *The Gate of the Hundred Sorrows*
25. DANTE · *Circles of Hell*
26. HENRY MAYHEW · *Of Street Piemen*
27. HAFEZ · *The nightingales are drunk*
28. GEOFFREY CHAUCER · *The Wife of Bath*
29. MICHEL DE MONTAIGNE · *How We Weep and Laugh at the Same Thing*
30. THOMAS NASHE · *The Terrors of the Night*
31. EDGAR ALLAN POE · *The Tell-Tale Heart*
32. MARY KINGSLEY · *A Hippo Banquet*
33. JANE AUSTEN · *The Beautifull Cassandra*
34. ANTON CHEKHOV · *Gooseberries*
35. SAMUEL TAYLOR COLERIDGE · *Well, they are gone, and here must I remain*
36. JOHANN WOLFGANG VON GOETHE · *Sketchy, Doubtful, Incomplete Jottings*
37. CHARLES DICKENS · *The Great Winglebury Duel*
38. HERMAN MELVILLE · *The Maldive Shark*
39. ELIZABETH GASKELL · *The Old Nurse's Story*
40. NIKOLAY LESKOV · *The Steel Flea*

41. HONORÉ DE BALZAC · *The Atheist's Mass*
42. CHARLOTTE PERKINS GILMAN · *The Yellow Wall-Paper*
43. C.P. CAVAFY · *Remember, Body . . .*
44. FYODOR DOSTOEVSKY · *The Meek One*
45. GUSTAVE FLAUBERT · *A Simple Heart*
46. NIKOLAI GOGOL · *The Nose*
47. SAMUEL PEPYS · *The Great Fire of London*
48. EDITH WHARTON · *The Reckoning*
49. HENRY JAMES · *The Figure in the Carpet*
50. WILFRED OWEN · *Anthem For Doomed Youth*
51. WOLFGANG AMADEUS MOZART · *My Dearest Father*
52. PLATO · *Socrates' Defence*
53. CHRISTINA ROSSETTI · *Goblin Market*
54. *Sindbad the Sailor*
55. SOPHOCLES · *Antigone*
56. RYŪNOSUKE AKUTAGAWA · *The Life of a Stupid Man*
57. LEO TOLSTOY · *How Much Land Does A Man Need?*
58. GIORGIO VASARI · *Leonardo da Vinci*
59. OSCAR WILDE · *Lord Arthur Savile's Crime*
60. SHEN FU · *The Old Man of the Moon*
61. AESOP · *The Dolphins, the Whales and the Gudgeon*
62. MATSUO BASHŌ · *Lips too Chilled*
63. EMILY BRONTË · *The Night is Darkening Round Me*
64. JOSEPH CONRAD · *To-morrow*
65. RICHARD HAKLUYT · *The Voyage of Sir Francis Drake Around the Whole Globe*
66. KATE CHOPIN · *A Pair of Silk Stockings*
67. CHARLES DARWIN · *It was snowing butterflies*
68. BROTHERS GRIMM · *The Robber Bridegroom*
69. CATULLUS · *I Hate and I Love*
70. HOMER · *Circe and the Cyclops*
71. D. H. LAWRENCE · *Il Duro*
72. KATHERINE MANSFIELD · *Miss Brill*
73. OVID · *The Fall of Icarus*
74. SAPPHO · *Come Close*
75. IVAN TURGENEV · *Kasyan from the Beautiful Lands*
76. VIRGIL · *O Cruel Alexis*
77. H. G. WELLS · *A Slip under the Microscope*
78. HERODOTUS · *The Madness of Cambyses*
79. *Speaking of Siva*
80. *The Dhammapada*